Hiram H McLane

The capture of the Alamo

a historical tragedy, in four acts, with prologue

Hiram H McLane

The capture of the Alamo
a historical tragedy, in four acts, with prologue

ISBN/EAN: 9783743303195

Manufactured in Europe, USA, Canada, Australia, Japa

Cover: Foto ©Andreas Hilbeck / pixelio.de

Manufactured and distributed by brebook publishing software
(www.brebook.com)

Hiram H McLane

The capture of the Alamo

To every lover of Liberty, having the right appreciation of the sacrifices made by men, in all ages of the world, to secure it for themselves and their fellow-men, this work is respectfully dedicated by

THE AUTHOR.

Preface.

THIS TRAGEDY was written to be placed upon the *boards*, and is now published to be sold for the purpose in part of raising funds to erect a suitable MONUMENT on the spot where they fell, to that band of noble men who sacrificed their lives for their country, on that memorable occasion, of which a very faint outline is herein given.

References will be found in the body of the work directing attention to corresponding ones at the end or back part, where will be found extracts from *Yoakum's History of Texas*, containing accounts of the scenes and incidents which have served as a foundation upon which to construct the work itself.

As a venture, the object is a laudable one. As to its merits, either as a literary production or a successful dramatic delineation, the success which may attend its presentations on the stage —should it be so fortunate as to ever get there— and the sale of the volume, will be the best criterions by which to judge; and to these tests it is now submitted, to stand or fall, as the case may be, by the

AUTHOR.

San Antonio, Texas.

Prologue.

The world in every age doth claim,
Its *heroes* who have died for fame ;
A Rome, a Greece, a Troy hath spread
A record broad of noble dead,
Who each one there his life laid down
For worldly honors and renown.
And our own Alamo doth claim
A list not known so well to fame,
But with the aid of HOMER's strain,
They would a place in it obtain.
Yet, what by pen we here record,
May still such place to them afford
As shall to you, in part portray,
The sacrifice they made that day,
When each one there his own life gave
To freedom for their country save.
Since, but for those who thus then fell,
None yet would there in freedom dwell ;
And, therefore, honor meet we'd pay
To all who fell upon that day.
And what shall here to you be shown,
Will hist'ry be together thrown.
Though in a fragmentary way,
Of what occurred from day to day,
As he, the *Arch Dictator* came.

A full surrender to him claim
'Till those, who rather chose to die,
Than to surrender or to fly,
Gave up their lives at most of cost
To his o'erwhelming storming host.

And this our purpose too we have,
Besides to honor those so brave;
By in this form to you to tell,
How Travis and his comrades fell;
To see if Shakspeare has a fame
To which no others may lay claim.
And if our style is somewhat quaint.
And neither gay nor grave does paint,
In tragic some, in comic more,
Not filled with with wit, nor yet with lore,
It does the trains of thought pursue.
As culled from facts of history through.
And may constructions bear, thus placed
By e'en those rules the most straight-laced.

And though to purpose first to tell
How Travis and his comrades fell,
We have the second added to;
As question put to each of you
We'll not for answer make demand.
'Till you have heard unto the end.

Dramatis Personæ.

ANTONIO LOPEZ DE SANTA ANNA.......................Dictator of Mexico

DON MARTIN PERFECTO COS...
    Brother-in-law to SANTA ANNA, and General in Mexican Army

GENERAL FELISOLA...⎫
GENERAL CASTRILLON...⎪
GENERAL RAMIREZ...⎪ Officers in
GENERAL SESMA...·...............⎬   the
GENERAL GAONA...⎪ Mexican Army
COLONEL ALMONTA..⎭

MRS. GAONA..Wife of General GAONA

MEXICAN SOLDIERS...

MAJOR NIXON..⎫
JUDGE FORBES..⎪
GOVERNOR VIESCA...⎬ Nacogdoches
DON IRALA...⎪
CITIZENS..⎭

W. B. TRAVIS, COLONEL COMMANDING...................⎫
COLONEL DAVID CROCKETT.................................⎪
COLONEL JAMES BOWIE..⎪
COLONEL J. B. BONHAM...⎪ Inmates
MAJOR EVANS..⎬   of
LIEUTENANT DICKINSON.....................................⎪ the Alamo
SCOUT AND SENTINEL..⎪
MRS. DICKINSON AND CHILD................................⎪
TWO MEXICAN WOMEN...⎪
NEGRO SERVANT TO TRAVIS................................⎭

THE CAPTURE OF THE ALAMO.

ACT I.

Scene I.—Gen. Gaona's quarters at Guerrero.
Mrs. Gaona seated, with book in hand.

[*Enter Santa Anna.*]

MRS. GAONA.

Why do you come here at this hour,
To honor bring me by your presence?
How knew you that I was alone;
And feared you not you'd meet my husband?

SANTA ANNA.

Nay, trust me; that I've guarded well
Against such chance of meeting,
For he a mission has away,
As he obeys my special orders.
To answer give you to the rest,
I've sought your presence now;
As first, I'm driven by desire
That hourly would bring me to you,
Since naught of rival you need fear,
Save and except my strong ambition.
And next, 'tis this does bring me here,
To all my plans to you unfold,
Since now I'm trusting none but you.

MRS. GAONA.

But why not seek one who can aid
To further on your plans thus formed?
A woman's sphere does ill become
Such grand designs.

SANTA ANNA.

Nay; I would not my honors share,
By joining with me others.
No; I am not in search of aid,
But only wish for confidence;
And since to woman that belongs—
At least when man does wish to place—
I come with mine, as with my heart,
Before I've done to you.

MRS. GAONA.

But pray, why not then go to her,
Who by the right of marriage vows
Will sharer be in all your honors,
And should, too, have your confidence.

SANTA ANNA.

Aye, we as children seek for toys,
And then in youth to fancies go,
And when to manhood first we come,
We still retain enough of each
That they do oft for us then form
What we accept as our ideals,
And which may all through life remain,
But only though as then in form,
But what our riper judgments claim
As meet for fit companionship.

Is of more solid substance formed
Than toys or fancies.
And whilst in her I see the one,
I find in full in you the other;
And so, I brought you my devotion,
And as you have accepted that,
I'd have go with'it, confidence.

MRS. GAONA.

Speak on. then, if to serve your will,
The purpose brings recital;
What ear I have for such high aims,
I will it lend unto you.

SANTA ANNA.

So far my cause is well in hand, (*a*)
The Congress does my will obey;
And all who would resist my power
Do keep their opposition close,
Or else have from the country fled,
Except these few in Texas.
Aye, there's my bosom friend, Zavalla, (*b*)
He to whom I owe my power;
And he would too have had me halt
And put a check to my ambition.
But then in haste I made him fly,
And when he'd fled I did pursue,
And do his capture yet demand.
Since favors done, nor friendships shall
My way to power supreme hedge up.
And as I've said except for Texas,
Which does still the standard raise
Of rank rebellion 'gainst my power,

I should in peace and quiet reign
Supreme o'er all the land.
For what of power that still does seem
To in the Congress yet remain,
Is but the merest sham ;
And when the plan which I've matured,
To be for future rule for Texas, (c)
Shall have been passed by them in form,
As I have deemed best it should be
For but prudential reasons,
I will in haste dismiss them then,
And will so rule that none shall dare
My right to rule to question.
For he, who would such rule assume,
Must have no sharer but his will;
And since I've willed that you should be
Made well acquaint with all my plans—
Thus guarding 'gainst e'en chance betrayal—
I will unto you make that known,
Of which by purpose I have willed
Shall be my future plan for Texas :
I have it written on this sheet,
That it may to my tools be sent
For their lank-formed endorsement.

[*He reads.*]

" To drive from that one province all
Who have assisted in the war,
As well as all of foreign-birth
Who do reside near to the coast,
Or on the borders of the neighboring nation.
And to remove into the Central States

Those who no part have taken in the war;
To make as void all sales and grants of land
Now owned by those who're not residing there;
And remove from Texas all who had not come
Into the province and enrolled,
In manner as prescribed by the nation's laws,
For colonists enacted.
To portion out amongst the soldiers
All those lands as of the parts the best;
Provided they will dwell thereon,
And then permit no one to settle there
Who is of Anglo American blood;
But sell the lands remaining—
To the French five million acres,
And to England's sons the same,
And to the Germans somewhat more.
Unto the Spanish-speaking subjects, without
    limit.
And for meeting all expenses of the war,
To make the Texans pay the same;
To satisfy the Indian claims,
And liberate all slaves brought to the province
And make of them good citizens."
Such is the plan that I've devised;
And I must, too, with all dispatch,
The same unto my minions send,
That I their sanction may obtain,
As I must yet, on vested rights
But tread with care, and lightly,
Lest I perchance too much arouse
True Anglo-Saxon blood.
For they whom I would thus prescribe
Have from their mothers' milk imbibed

2

Too much of freedom to submit
To aught not backed with legal forms;
But when 'tis vested thus, and sent
To be enforced by writ of court,
Then shall a force be brought to bear
Which shall the country of them rid;
And I may then in safety reign
O'er all the land supreme.

MRS. GAONA.

As nature doth the fawn protect
By want of scent from prowling beast,
'Till it hath strength and fleetness gained
To its pursuers far outstrip—
So hath a prescience been thy guide
In thus maturing all thy plans,
As their success thus far doth show,
And which does future promise give
Of grand results in termination.

SANTA ANNA.

But hold! one act I've not disclosed, (*d*)
Which by decree I had them make,
Which will the "*Gringo * Dogs*" make flee
Like hunted wolves before the hounds,
Or battle do, e'en unto death.
Which last would meet my wishes most,
Since them I'll meet with convict force, (*e*)
And deem them dead as but good riddance—
And therefore it is meet I should
Make all due haste, and get to Bexar

---

* *Gringos.*—An appellation given to the Americans by the Mexican in retaliation for their being called *Greasers* by them; and the signification is much the same.

Before its purport shall be known
To other portions of the State,
And they be roused to their defence,
As I did due precautions take
To have it reach there in advance
Of my own coming by the space
Of but a few days, at the most.
So that they cannot notice give
To other points, from which there may
Unto them succor there be sent,
As with my force I can, with ease,
Their present force o'erwhelm;
But lest they through some other way
The purport of it do obtain,
I must my stay at once cut short
And be away, as it is better they should not
From Bexar escape, and join their force
To those of others farther east.
That act to which I have referred
Is that in which it is decreed
That all of foreign birth who're found
In open arms against me, shall
Be dealt with as with pirates.
And if such shall be strictly done,
Good riddance shall be got of all
Who would my peaceful rule obstruct.

MRS. GAONA.

Your plans do like the winged birds fly
From point to point, with so much ease
That none so wary found may be
As of themselves, to thwart them.
And though of pride my boast may seem,

I can but boast it with a pride,
That I have been so worthy thought
As to be by you so far trusted.

SANTA ANNA.

None fears the brink, when cliff's not seen;
Nor shuns abyss, when not exposed;
And they but fear a tyrant's will,
To whom that tyrant's power's disclosed.
  [*The bugle-call heard in the distance.*]
Aye, there's the bugle-call, and I must away,
And to the review.
                    [*Exit Santa Anna.*]

MRS. GAONA.

Aye, he but little knows of woman's will;
He did discourse of confidence.
Do tyrants seek such? Then 'tis well;
He'll find his in me not misplaced
For weal to those he seeks to rule,
But to his own high aims, a bar.
But I must play my part with care,
And shield myself and husband;
For, whilst I seem to him to yield,
He'll not suspect our purpose,
And thus we can our plans pursue
To render service to our friends,
Whom he has said alone do check
Now place to his ambition.
I must my husband, too, acquaint
Of this, his coming and his plans,
That we together counsel take,
That he, perchance, be thwarted.

Scene II.—A large hall in the house of Maj.
Nixon, at Nacogdoches, with citizens assembled
to entertain with a feast Don Augustine Viesca,
the deposed Governor of Coahuila and Texas, and
his secretary, Don Irala, who had escaped from
Mexico and sought an asylum there. A table is
set with dishes and the guests seated, with Maj.
Nixon at the head, the Governor on the right,
and Irala next. (*f*)

MAJOR NIXON.

Whilst here, awaiting that the servants shall
    bring in
And fill these empty plates with savory viands,
'Tis well we should by other feast be fed;
As all our minds and hearts do hunger,
And would e'en fain be fed
By that which would impart more strength
    unto them ˙
Than the savory viands we've prepared, to
    make the feast
In honor of these here, our guests, shall do un-
    to our bodies.
The threatened famine of the heart and mind,
Which at this hour does make us lank and lean,
Is that destruction of our chartered rights, (*g*)
In superceding all those guarantees of '24,
Thus blasting hopes of peace and quiet
Round our own hearth-stones;
By that dictatorship and centralizing power,
Which all the States save this, our own,
It ready holds in thraldom; (*a*)
And at this moment threatens us, alike,

With chains and slavery.
For what besides a *peonage* can come to us,
If tamely waiting for that coming horde,
Of those, the creatures of that central power
In form of standing army, (*a*)
Made up of minions but to do a tyrant's bid-
    ding?
And what shall then become of all the rights
Assured by acts and laws in aid of coloniza-
    tion, (*k*)
And contracts made thereunder? (*u*)
What says our worthy guest,
Has he fit meat with which to feed us?

DON VIESCA.

That savory dish of most of which I'd spread
    your board,
Is that one purpose which does all your actions
    strongly mark,
Of firm resistance to that central power,
And which alone can lead to such results
As shall the least of promise give of future
    fatness.
The purpose is, as it to you I would impart—
And which by chance I did obtain—
Through plan submitted from Guerrero
By that tyrant, Santa Anna, to his pliant Con-
    gress,
And the confirmation of the which, too, by them
Has the more become assured
Since they have shown themselves to be
The creatures of his power,
Set up, in forms of law, to do his bidding. (*a*)

The plan, I say, thus formed,
And but submitted for their sanction,
That the veil, though thin,
Of seeming grant of power
May to you e'en seem thus confirmed,
Is to drive from that province all
Who have assisted in the war,
As well as all of foreign birth
Who do reside near to the coast,
Or on the borders of the neighboring nation;
And to remove into the Central States
Those who no part have taken in the war,
To make as void all sales and grants of land
Now owned by those who're not residing there;
And then remove from Texas
All who had not come
Into the province and enrolled,
In manner as provided by the nation's laws,
For colonists enacted.
To portion out amongst the soldiers
All those lands as of the parts the best,
Provided, they will dwell thereon.
And then, permit no one to settle there
Who is of Anglo-American blood;
But sell the lands remaining—
To the French, five millions acres,
And to England's sons, the same,
And to the Germans, somewhat more.
Unto the Spanish-speaking subjects, without
limit.
And for meeting all expenses of the war,
To make the Texans pay the same.

To satisfy the Indian claims ;
And liberate all slaves brought to the province
And make of them good citizens." (*c*)

Such is the dish they are preparing for your
    palates ;
And, but for efforts strong and joint,
They yet will thrust it down your throats.

[*Enter Citizen.*]

CITIZEN.

I come to bring you tidings of good news unto
    our cause.
A chief of note his presence presses on our
    threshold now,
And even at this moment enters full within
    the town,
Enroute to active scenes of warfare,
Where his former prestige and his present
    valor
May be placed within the scale
To aid in bringing down the poise
Upon the side of our wronged rights.
And I am here to give you notice that no other
Than the noted son of Tennessee,
The daring DAVID CROCKETT,
Does our town thus honor with his presence,
And our cause does wish to strengthen
By the making it his own. (*f*)

MAJOR NIXON.

This news comes, at this juncture of affairs,
To bear with pleasing sense upon our minds,
And lift from them somewhat the weight

Which the recital to us made
Of plans and purpose of the central power
To subjugate us to its will, did thereon place,
And it is well that we have been assembled here
As we the better may him show without delay
A due respect unto his coming.
And now, with full consent—
As it I know I have of all those present—
I will him bid unto the feast,
That we may gain, from his own lips,
The causes moving to his actions,
And perchance to learn from him
Of others being like-minded,
Who yet will follow on, to swell
The number of our scanty forces;
And I therefore pray you bid him enter,
And let us his first coming greet
In fitting style, by rising to our feet,
And, with the sound of three good rousing
    cheers,
To make the hall reverberate. (*f*)

[*Exit one of the company, who returns with
Crockett, when he is greeted with three cheers,
and is placed in front of Viesca and to the left
of Nixon.*]

MAJOR NIXON.

Thrice welcome to the feast our cheers hath
    made you;
And not unto our feast alone, but to our cause,
Since we have been advised 'tis it
Hath thus you brought into our borders,

And we, before we order that these dishes shall
    be filled
With meats, to make of body cheer,
Do beg you to recount—if so it please you—
The reasons for your coming;
And, too, advise us of that state
In which our cause is held
Within the land from whence you came,
And what of others, if such there be,
Who, having heard of our great straits,
And having deemed our cause as just,
Have purposed too, themselves to place
Within the scale, which right and justice hold,
And with us, aid in bringing down the poise
To answer to our just demands.
Our guests, to whom we first to honor here
    were met,
And who that honor now will with you share,
Are with us joined,
And are like sufferers with ourselves,
In wrongs inflicted.
Since Don Viesca, he who does you there con-
    front,
And with whom I would have you made ac-
    quaint,
Did for adherence to the right,
The tyrant's power feel,
And was from his high office forced,
And by his daring only did escape,
And reached by stratagem these shores, (*h*)
A fit companion only having in Irala,
He upon his right, and being then his secretary,
And unto whom I would you, too, present,

So that in future you may know each other
As but worthy workers in a common cause.
And so, in your recital here, you none will have
Save those who're linked in like strong bond
Of common interest.
Speak on, then, if it please you to address us
    now,
Whilst we shall list'ners be.

CROCKETT.

Friends and feller citizens :
Yer has struk me rite this time, yer did,
As yer see I ar bin usenter this kinder thing
For fourteen yar in old Tennersee,
And in congress yer see.
For yer see ther nabers arl reck'nd
As I war ther best coon hunter any whar round,
I could also hunt out the rascallertys
They had hearn sumhow or anuther
War gwine on in Washinton.
And so, yer see, they stuk me up to run
Agin sum on yer hiferluten city chaps,
And, arltho they could tarlk
Like hail fallin on a board pile,
And use slathers o' big words,
Yet the nabers arl thort
They war not my match
In huntin out things.
And tharfore they sent me ter Washinton
To try ter hunt out ther rascallory things done
    thar.
Wall, when I got thar,
I went rite ter work ter see what I could do,

And I scented round, and scented round,
Like old Tige, my best coon dorg;
But I couldn't find nuthin but a cold trail,
And which allers run rite inter ther same hole,
And that war strate throo
Ther treasury house door, it war.
But when I got in thar,
Arl war as quiet as death thar,
And yer wouldn't have thort,
Ter have seed them chaps in thar,
That anything wrong had bin done thar
Since ther old house war built.
So I kept my eye skinned
Arl thro ther time I war thar,
And just afore my second term war up
I struk a fresh trail,
And cum home brim full of fight for anuther
    trial,
And I torld my nabers
If tha would jest send me back agin,
That I knowd I could cotch ther old fox,
With arl ther little ones,
And ther coons besides, ther next time.
But ther fellers when ther found
I war on ther hot trail,
Tha bought up arl ther noospapers,
And hired arl ther blab-mouthed fellers in ther
    country
Ter go round mongst my nabers,
And tell them arl kind 'er cock and bull stories,
And when I found how ther cat war gwine ter
    jump,
I jest torld my nabers

COL. DAVID CROCKETT.

That if ther war gwine ter listen to all ther
    stuff
Them fellers war gittin thro them,
And did n't send me back ter Washinton,
That then ther might arl go ter —
Wal, yer knos, ter that bad place —
And I would cum ter Texas.
For yer see when I war in Washinton,
. I hearn so much
About the way Mexerco war treatin' Texas,
I would have cum rite off
Ter have helped whip her outen her boots;
But then yer see
I wanted ter first foller up
Ther hot trail I had found;
But when my nabers arl went back on me,
And sent ther 'tother feller ter Washinton, yer
    see.
I skipped rite out for these diggins.
And har I ar now, jest ready ter pitch in
And lick ther blue blazes outen old Mexerco,
In less time ner it usened ter take
My old dorg, Towser,
Ter kill er baby coon in his best days.
And now, I want yer ter show me ther way
To ther biggest coon fite thars gwine ter be.
As for them other fellers,
What war talkin er bout cummin,
They were too slow coaches for me,
And I would n't wait for 'em, so I would n't;
But I reckon as how,
There'll be a rite smart sprinkle on 'em
Along arter a while.

And now, that ther trail ar hot,
Let me go thro' ther motions ter onct,
So that I can go havers with yer
In dividin ther game.
Bring on yer book,
And let me stick my fist rite ter it ter onct,
And then I shall be ready to cut ther eye-teeth,
By puttin' ther tiger four over ther eyes, as big
   'as a bar's foot,
Or whoever will dare to raise a finger
'Gainst our Texas.

MAJOR NIXON.

Come, let us first partake of the repast, wich
   I fear
Has ready grown sodden,
By reason of our long delay
In the issuance of our orders for its serving.

CROCKETT.

No, no! Old DAVY CROCKETT never yet let his
   dorgs loose
With stomachs filled with nabers' food
And then demanded share o' game.
No, no; let me first go through ther motions,
And then I'll jine yer in ther feast.

MAJOR NIXON.

Away, then, to the proper office we will go,
And let his wishes thus be met. (*f*)

[*A scene is drawn, showing the office of Judge Forbes with the Judge seated at a table with writing material. Enter Nixon, Crockett and citizens.*]

MAJOR NIXON.

Though oft on errands like we've come,
We yet have not before, like this,
Been called to leave a feast unserved,
And yet prepared and left unserved
For reasons strange as this has been.
Since this, our guest whom we have called,
Does so refuse to join with us
Until he does allegiánce bear unto our cause;
And thus we've brought him unto you,
That you may in a proper form
A legal subject of him make,
That thus he may, as he desires,
Be equal with us in demands of rights,
As well as sharer in our fasts and feasts.

JUDGE FORBES.

It is his purpose, then, to take the oath
That's been by our own chiefs prescribed?
If such his wish, 'tis well; the form is this:
I, A. B., of my own free will, and with intent
And purpose full, and knowledge clear
Of what I'm thus required to do,
By this, my act, do here renounce
All form of liege I e'er have borne,
Or yet do bear,
Unto the lands from whence I came,
And true allegiance thus assume
Unto that form that's been prepared
For rule of Texas.
Or such other form as shall in future be decreed
By those who shall be then her rulers.
Dost sign?

3

CROCKETT.

Old coon, I recken, now, you'll hardly get me
    thar;
The trail I'm on does only have the scent of
    a Republic. (*f*)

MAJOR NIXON.

How then; shall not the change be made
To suit his wishes;
Hath not our chiefs so thus decreed?
For who among them,
If himself thus brought to make the choice,
Would not demand the same;
And who among them
Deems aught else but a Republic possible?

JUDGE FORBES.

Then let it so be done;
The change I'll make, and let him sign. (*f*)

     [*He changes.*]

The change is made, and thus it reads:
" For rule of Texas, or such other form
As shall in future be decreed
By those who shall be then her rulers,
If that form be a Republic."

CROCKETT.

That ars it now; that's ther trail I'm runnin' on,
And let me stick my fist ter onct ter it.

[*Crockett signs, and Judge Forbes, looking at
the signature, says:*]

JUDGE FORBES.

What! art thou he of whom we've heard so oft,
As in the wilds of Tennessee
Thou didst the game with hounds pursue;
And when to Congress thou were sent,
The hall was filled with thy quaint speech,
And with thy rustic tales did all enchain?
Then welcome to our cause,
Since thy valor, like thy speech.
Hath thus far made thee famous;
And may thy acts of prowess in our cause
Not dim the present lustre of thy name?

MAJOR NIXON.

And now unto the feast we'll go.
And of its savory meats partake
With relish, whetted sharp with fasting.

ACT II.

SCENE I.— Gen. GAONA's quarters, in camp between Guerrero and San Antonio. Present— Gen. and Mrs. GAONA; the latter attired in male apparel, and in the act of adjusting her hat.

MRS. GAONA.

How think you, General, will that do
To pass me for a trooper?

GENERAL GAONA.

You have with skill your sex disguised,
But I shall fear me you will lack
A proper soldier's bearing.
Still, to our patron saint belongs
The task alone of guarding you.
But you must bear the drill in mind,
As I have taught it unto you,
Of how you will approach the guard,
And for the day the word is "*Hondo*,"
And you know the *rendezvous*,
Where you'll find our friend, the scout,
And, with a prayer unto the saint,
You must in haste away,
As it is meet our friends should know,
Not only of his rapid coming,
But the tyrant's threats, as well;
So, quick, away.

[*Exit Mrs. Gaona.*]

And I must to the vulture go,
To learn his plans as best I may,
That I may shield the threatened prey.

Scene II.—Travis' quarters at San Antonio.
Travis sitting at a table with papers, &c. upon it.

[*Enter Officer of the Guard.*]

OFFICER.

Whilst out remounting guard,
From which I've just returned,
We captured quite a prize for us,
In person one of whom I've oft,
Heard you make special mention,
And he will likewise to our cause
Be quite an acquisition.
And I have ordered, that as soon
As he shall finish the repast
Of which he sorely stood in need,
That to your quarters he be brought,
As he the wish did so express,
And it did with my will accord,
As I assured it would to you
Be likewise, too, most pleasing.

TRAVIS.

My wish thy will would sorely press;
To have at once you make it known,
To whom you do by speech refer,
As queries rise which will not down,
To vex my anxious spirit.
I therefore pray you, not to wait
His coming; to announce his name.
If one before that I have known,

I then the better shall him greet,
And not appear confused, or rude.

OFFICER.

I hear the sound of steps approach,
And he does hither come.

[*Enter Crockett, and the officer escorts him to
Travis, who rises.*]

This is he, of whom I spake,
And that to each the other know,
I would, when hands are joined by you,
A CROCKETT's say a TRAVIS' holds,
And so your hands you may thus join,
And by them thus be made acquaint.

[*They join their hands.*]

TRAVIS.

Thrice welcome do we make you here:
With hand, and heart, and speech,
Since naught, we know, but our just cause
Did thus you bring to us.

[*They let go each others' hands.*]

CROCKETT.

Wall, now, Kernel, yer rite thar;
For, yer see, when I war in Washinton,
And arter I'd cum home ter old Tennersee,
I'd hearn a good deal tarlked about
Ther coon fight yer fellers were havin'
With old Santer Anner and his pack outen har.
And, yer see, when my nabers arl went back
    on me,
And wouldn't send me back ter Washinton,

To foller up ther hot trail
I had found when I war thar,
As I torld them other fellers,
In that other town thar,
Whar they war havin' a dinner
Without anything ter eat when I cum thar,
And whar ther wanted me ter swar I would fite
Fer a king, or any other kind of a feller
Ther wanted ter put up fer a figer head
Fer a new government fer Texas;
But, yer bet, Kernel, I war too old er coon
Ter be caught in that trap, so 1 war,
And so I torld ther feller,
What war bossin' ther job,
That ther only trail I war willin' ter run on
War a good old Republic,
Like ther one I war usenter.
So, yer see, anuther feller said he didn't see
Why I couldn't have my way 'bout it,
As he know'd yer fellers outen har
Wanted it that ar way, too.
And yer see that other feller what war bossin' it
He changed it rite er way, he did,
And I stuk my fist ter it ter onct;
And arter that, don't yer think
We arl went and sot down ter ther grub
They'd had in ther pots cookin' ever since
    mornin';
Fer, yer see, ther war gwine ter give ther grub
Ter two blasted big-bug Mexicans thar;
But, yer see, when I cum thar
They cheer'd, and cheer'd, and cheer'd.

And yer bet I put on my Washinton manners,
And strutted 'round purty big like,
And used my best dicshunary.
Wall, I've kinder gotten off ther trail a leetle,
But I recken as how I'll get back agin
To whar I was sayin'
That when my nabers arl went back on me,
And would n't send me back ter Washinton,
I torld them they might arl go ter —
Wall, Kernel, yer knows whar that ar—
It's ther bad place, Kernel.
Wall, as I war sayin',
I torld them ther might arl go thar,
And I would go ter Texas, yer see ;
And so, yer see, har I ar, rite har, Kernel.
Jist as good as my word, Kernel.
Fer, yer see, old DAVY CROCKETT
Never yet went back on his word ;
No, Kernel, for his motter allers war,
" Be shore yer rite, then go ahead."
And now, if yer got any fitin' ter do,
Jist bring on yer fellers,
And I'll lick ther flints fer 'em
In less time ner it usenter take
Old Towser ter whip er baby coon
In his best days, so I will, Kernel.

TRAVIS.

Well, Colonel, I guess you'll have a chance
To show your skill in that line ;
And now I'll take a turn around with you,
And show you how we live here,
And the sights in general.

Scene III.—Travis' quarters; present, Travis and others (his staff.)

TRAVIS.

What! No news yet from scouts dispatched,
To but confirm, or yet disprove
The rumors of the foe's approach?
No wary fox e'er play'd his game of tack
With more of skill than they their parts
As spies and scouts do play,
And therefore it can bode no ill to them.

[*Enter Sentinel.*]

SENTINEL.

There's one without, who came in haste,
And makes demand to be brought in,
As he an urgent message has,
And therefore illy brooks delay:
But thus your will, and so your orders,
And I had him stand in waiting,
Till you bid me let him enter.

TRAVIS.

Send him in; it must be one for whom we look;
And bid him come without delay.

[*Exit Sentinel.*]

Ah! Now our tingling ears shall catch
The truth, no doubt, since neither would return
Unladen with the news so needed to be borne.

[*Enter Scout.*]

TRAVIS.

What news dost bring?
What of the rumors that have filled the air,
And rang, like chimes of church bells,
On our ears,
Of that vast host, led by that chief,
With heart so blackened with deceit,
And hands filled full of craftiness;
Who, while the smile was on his lips,
And protestations on his breath,
Of warm attachment
To that compact made in '24,
Was seeking its full overthrow?
Come, now, the burden of thy message quick
    unload,
And thus our ears relieve, with its recital.

SCOUT.

Those swift-winged rumors,
Which, so like the birds of passage,
Following fast within the other's track,
Did reach your ears in flocks,
Were burdened with much more of truth
Than our defenceless state, I fear,
Shall make it pleasing to your ears,
To have confirmed.
For he, the chieftain comes —
As did those rumors have it —
With a well appointed force,
And numbered by the thousands; (c)
And yet, with more from other points
To join him still,

Thus making up the flower and chief
Of his, so boastful, followers;
And even, at this moment, does
His van-guard press upon us,
With the main force
But a few leagues distant:
With purpose full, to make that victory void,
So nobly gained, when MILAM fell; (*i*)
And wipe from off his kinsman's valor, (*e*)
The stain thus made, by his surrender.
And farther boasting, he does threat
To drive from off the sacred soil,
Or put to sword, those "*Gringo Dogs*"—
As he doth please to name those
Who were 'ticed to enter on,
And drive from thence the savage foe, (*j*)
And break the soil, to make them homes —
Fair, smiling homes — and 'ticed thus,
By those pledges made, in form of law, (*k*)
Which should be yet most sacred;
But which, through want of faith well kept,
Are by him disregarded;
And which do make the basis now,
Of this, our cause.
This much I learned from one
Unto our cause attached,
Though with the foe in favor,
Who, by appointment made,
Did from the chieftain's quarters come,
Where council, then, was held.

TRAVIS.

'Tis well; his arrogance and boastful will
Shall serve to lead him in that trap
Wherein unwary birds are caught.
Such is the will of Him who guides
When wrong against the right is waged,
And plighted faith is broken.
For, like that boasting prince who fled before
Those mystic sounds, borne on the breeze, .
When he had pitched against that chosen band,
He too, shall of the fears born of the right,
With conscience lighted up with wrong,
When magic power of our strong arms
Shall their full force of light
Upon the canvass throw,
Betake himself to whence he came,
Or else be made to bite the dust.
And each, his craven follower, shall
A bullet feel, from certain aim
Of some one trusty piece
Held by our patriot hands.
And now, let Bonham, Bowie, Crockett, Evans,
All be called.
That we may hold a council here forthwith.

[*Exit one of his staff.*]

TRAVIS, (turning to Scout.)

And you may your own quarters seek,
And when refreshed, with food and sleep,
Then, to the foe return again,
That, watching, you may bring us news
Of all his movements.

[*Exit Scout.*]

[*Enter Bonham, Bowie, Crockett and Evans,
with Bowie carried in on a cot.*]

TRAVIS, (TO BOWIE.)

How now, Colonel?
It is well you're convalescing;
And the news brought by our scout
May serve the purpose by far better
Than either splints or sticking-plaster,
To keep your fractured bones in place,
And hasten on the knitting process.

[*To all.*]

I've called you all unto this council,
As one despatched but two days since
Does, on return, bring back the news
That those swift rumors, which the air did fill
Of rapid coming of the foe,
Was not without foundation,
And also says that even now
His force does number thousands,
With more yet on the way to join him;
And that the lion doth his mane, too, shake,
And in his growls are mingled threats
Of flight by us, or slaughter.
What say you?
Shall we thus his gage take up,
And waiting here, prepare to meet him?
Or shall we, while we yet have time,
Before his coming, fly?

[*Turning to Bowie.*]

What say you, Colonel?

BOWIE.

My fractured limb, with bones unknit,
And, therefore, lack of power of motion,
Unfits me quite, by force of arms,
Such threat to bring to naught;
But, what of power or skill I have,
'Tis yet my will to consecrate,
And I would counsel, not to fly,
But here prepare to meet him.

TRAVIS.

What is the counsel CROCKETT gives?
Is it, the " dogs of war let slip;"
And as, when in his native wilds,
The game to put at bay?
Or does he counsel, that with leash in hand,
We do retrace the trail we came,
And leave the foe the field?

CROCKETT.

Old Towser never yet gave false alarm,
And when he opened on ther track
We know'd ther game war thar,
And when they came in at ther death,
The nabers allers found
That CROCKETT, too, war thar;
And since ther scout, like Towser, tells
That now the game ar thar,
No coward thort shall make him fear
Ter meet ther lion in ther way.

TRAVIS.

To counsel farther, there's no need,
Since it is plain, we're all agreed,
And to at once, to perfect plans,
That we may here resist the foe,
'Tis meet we should dispatches send
To those, our chiefs, for so much aid
As they may have to send to us:
Which by swift courier we will do.

ACT III.

SCENE I.—Gen. GAONA's quarters at San Antonio. Mrs. G. arranging articles upon a table.

[*Enter Santa Anna.*]

SANTA ANNA.

'Tis my good fortune thus to find you,
As I purposed, and alone.

MRS. GAONA.

Pray, to what saint does thanks belong
For this, thy coming?

SANTA ANNA.

The clinging vine to sturdy oak
Does no more seek for there a stay
Than man his heart to woman brings,
For sharer in its burdens.

MRS. GAONA.

Like fledgling in the downy nest,
That heeds the parent's call,
To its accustomed food receive,
So I, with waiting ears, respond
To your proposed recital.

SANTA ANNA.

Shall I the world's forced rules so honor
As that I shall make a demand
Of this small handful here of men
That they shall unto me surrender?
Such "*Gringo Dogs*" deserve not such
High honors thus, at hands of mine;
But nay, I may not well bring down
Upon my head one blow e'en yet.
I fear the time is not quite here
When I the world may disregard;
And therefore, I would council hold,
With those around me,
That I, at least with seeming, may
Submit somewhat unto their will.
What! does your woman's wit, too, sanction
Such, my purpose?

MRS. GAONA.

The eagle, as he soars aloft,
With anxious gaze doth scan
The earth, spread out thus to his gaze,
To see thereon his prey;
But only when he feels 'tis sure
Will he descent upon it make.

SANTA ANNA.

Ah! Then you'd have me council call?

MRS. GAONA.

As you do fear, the time's not here
To place your will 'gainst all the world.
You have yourself made such decision.

4

SANTA ANNA.

I illy brook this, my restraint,
Which I have forced upon myself.
As born in me of prudence.
But it shall be but for a season,
For soon I'll burst its bonds,
And give free rein unto my will.
But for the present, I'll obey
This self-imposed restraint.
And council call.

[*Exit Santa Anna.*]

MRS. GAONA.

Is this the road that ever leads
To such, ambition's height?
And can vain man, with e'en his greeds,
E'er tread it with delight?
Are not the steeps, o'er which to tread,
With so much danger fraught?
Though gaining goal, to which he's led,
Is not the height too dearly sought?
And then, when grasping in his hand,
The prize by him thus won,
He finds not spot secure to stand,
But must the race still onward run.
Then, who would wish to play such part?
Or seek to tyrant be?
Ah! None but such as have a heart
From milk of human kindness free.

Scene II.—Santa Anna's quarters at San Antonio, with seats arranged for holding a council: present, Santa Anna.

SANTA ANNA.

Aye! Prithee now if she the one,
Of all the world, I've dared to trust,
Should recreant prove, and me expose?
But then, the point 'tis guarded well;
She could alone, *her* word, then place
Within the scale, beside my own.
But, pshaw! what thought is this obtrudes
To thus disquiet?
Would not the nation laugh to scorn
Such speech, but yet half uttered?
But here they come, and now, once more,
My struggling pride be-still.
The days of thy forced surveilance
Shall soon be passed.

[*Enter Felisola, Gaona, Sesma, Almonte and Cos*]

SANTA ANNA.

It is my will, as doubtless hath
Been unto each of you conveyed,
To council hold here at this hour,
As to the course I shall pursue
Towards the foe,
Who does himself, within those walls,
With arrogance, now dare set up
The rights of Christian warfare.
For with decree, from supreme power, (*a*)
They should be treated as but pirates,
And should be hanged
Without the rights, e'en of the church.
What say you? Shall I then extend
Unto them what the world does claim

To be their due in warfare?
Or shall they, by our own decree,
Be brought unto its bar?

> [*Turning to Felisola.*]

What say you, General?

FELISOLA.

'Tis but to answer to your will,
That I would essay now to speak,
And would concur in what you say
In so far as to what you've said
As to that one inherent right,
That we would have
To them to treat, as being bound by that decree
Which our own nation's sovereign power
Has deemed it fit,
By their own will to promulgate.
But, as this council you have called,
Does seeming right unto them give,
At least within your own great mind,
Else council would not thus be called,
A due regard for such might say
That prudence is the better way;
And since no harm can to our cause
From such delay, at least, arise,
I counsel give that we obey
The rule the world has given us,
And send a flag, with a demand
They do at once surrender.

SANTA ANNA.

Would others speak, or is the sense
Already reached of what you'd say?

And shall I send in a demand
That they to me shall thus surrender?

GENERAL GAONA.

If council hath by you been called
To pass upon these rebels' rights,
I counsel that they've ready passed
Beyond all claim the world does place
Within the scale that justice holds,
When in defiance of the will
The nation has at large expressed,
They would their own small wills set up,
And then demand their recognition. (*k*)
And I would, therefore, hold them subject
To the force of that decree.
Such is my counsel.

SANTA ANNA.

If none do farther wish to speak,
And it be left with me to say,
The wise suggestion that was made,
That we shall lose not by delay,
And farther yet, that two sides are,
Or have been made by me, to it,
I therefore will that there be sent
A flag, with bearer of demand
For unreserved and full surrender. (*l*)
And let it so, at once, be done.
And send a copy, too, along, of that decree,
That they be made to understand
That what they choose to disregard
Is clothed with power, yet, in the land.

SCENE III.—TRAVIS' quarters. TRAVIS seated
at a table.

[*Enter Crockett as Officer of the Day.*]

CROCKETT.

Wall, Kernel, what does yer think?
Arter I had put ther boys out on stake-rope,
As these 'ere chaps outen 'ere carls it,
But we'uns carls it picketern, in old Tennersee,
They hollered ter me ter cum thar,
And when I got thar, what der yer think I
    found thar?
Why, Kernel, it war one o' them blasted
    Greaser chaps,
Carryin' a stik with er white rag on it. (*l*)
And when I axed him what he wanted thar,
He said he wanted ter see ther feller
What war bossin' this 'ere layout;
And I torld him I war bossin' ther job
Jist then myself, I war;
And yer had orter have seed him look at me,
    Kernel,
As much as ter say:
"I ar not lookin' fer your sort."
And then he said he war wantin' ter see ther
    big boss;
And what der yer think I torld him then, Ker-
    nel?
Why, I torld him I reck'ned as how
Yer had sumthin' else ter do
Bersides list'nin' ter ther gab o' chaps o' his
    sort,
But if he had anerthing ter say
Ter us fellers over har, he could say rite on,

As I reck'ned I could stand ter listen ter ther
    stuff
He war wantin' ter get through him.
And, arter that, he opened ther kivers ter his
    bread basket,
And he got throo him that old Santer Anner
    had torld him
Ter cum rite over har, and tell arl us coons
Ter cum right down outen ther tree, ter onct,
Or he would do, as my old friend, Captain
    Scott, o' Varmount,
Usenter do, jist grin us down;
And I tell yer, Kernel,
The Captain allers brot 'em, when he tuk a
    sot at 'em.
And what does yer think, Kernel, I torld him?
Why, I torld him jist what I torld
My old nabers, in Tennersee,
When ther wouldn't send me back ter Wash-
    inton:
That ter tell old Santer that he might go ter—
Wall, its ther bad place, yer knows, Kernel—
That as fer me, I war one coon
That war not cumin' down
Outen ther tree fer sich chaps as him.
That so far as I war concarned, if he wanted me
He would have ter cum over har and take me.
As fer ther rest o' yer fellers,
If yer wanted ter cum down,
And sneak over thar, like whipped dorgs,
Yer mite do it; but as fer me,
I war n't gwine ter do it, fer sich chaps as him.
Ner a hundred more like him, so I war n't.

Wall, what der yer think he said then, Kernel?
Why, he said I orter to cum over
And tell yer 'bout it, anerhow.
So I torld him I would do that much
Fer old Santer, anerhow,
As I never seed an old, broken down,
And superannerated coon dorg,
But what war good for sumthin',
If it war only ter eat up
Ther old scraps lyin' round like;
And I thort, maber so, old Santer
War as good as one o' them;
And he said, "much obliged,"
Or sumthin' like it.
And I left, and cum rite off har,
And now I ar har, Kernel;
And if yer got anerthing to say,
Its yer say, Kernel.

TRAVIS.

Well, Colonel, I guess in your way,
You represented the sentiments of us all,
And if he didn't understand it,
He will soon do so, as it is my orders
That a single shot be fired (*l*)
In the direction of Santa Anna's quarters.
That is all the answer I have to make
To his demand; and you will see
That the order is complied with.

CROCKETT.

Yer bet yer bottom dollar, Kernel,
I'll see that ar thing done;
And, blast his old hide,

If I could knock ther hind sites offen him,
With that ar ball, I should be monstrous glad,
Now mind I tell yer, Kernel.
Good day, Kernel.

[*Crockett turns to go, but puts his hand in the
bosom of his hunting shirt, and turns quickly
around, having in his hand a paper, and says:*]

Blast my buttons, Kernel,
But I cum near fergettin' this 'ere thing,
I had stuk in my bosom fer safe keepin',
As that ar Greaser chap said ter gin it ter yer,
As it mout be of some use ter yer:
So, har it ar, Kernel, maber so,
Yer can do sumthin' with it.

[*Saying which, he hands to Travis, who takes
and looks at it, and says:*]

TRAVIS.

Hah! That foul decree,
And to be treated but as pirates;
Such is its terms.
And does he think to frighten us to terms,
By sending this along with his demand.

[*Crushing the paper in his hand, he extends
toward Crockett.*]

Here, put it in the cannon's mouth,
And let the powder,
That shall take unto his ears our answer,
Also take unto him this, his argument,
With which he would enforcement make
Of his demand.

[*Crockett takes and looking at it.*]

CROCKETT.

Does yer wish that this 'ere be made patchin uv
Fer ther ball, Kernel? If that's what yer wants,
Yer bet, Kernel, Betsy here
      [Holding up his rifle.]
Can send it ter him as strate as a die, Kernel.
Yer see she war gin ter me,
As yer knows, Kernel,
By them fellers in Philerdelpher thar,
When I war makin' ther tower
O' them ar Northern States, as one o' them
Honorable members from Tennersee;
And yer had orter have hearn me speechifien
    ter 'em,
So yer had ort, Kernel,
When ther gin her ter me,
And yer bet, Kernel, I ar killed many a bar
    with her, too.
And, as I war sayin' ter yer,
If yer wants this 'ere made patchin uv,
And sent back ter old Santer,
Yer bet, Kernel, Betsy's what can do it;
And if yer'll jist say ther word,
I'll put it right dab in, now,
And if he'll show a patch o' his old carcass
As big as a squirrel's ear, blast me
If I don't put ther ball rite dab thar,
Patchin' and all, so I will, Kernel.

TRAVIS.

Well, Colonel, you can either put it in the
    cannon's mouth,
Or use it for patching for Betsy, as you like.

As for the effect he hoped for in sending it here,
He has counted without his host this time;
And as before ordered, you will see
That the single shot is fired
In the direction of his quarters,
As all the answer I have still to give
To his demand.

CROCKETT.

Yer bet, Kernel, I'll see that ar thing done.
Now, good day, Kernel.

SCENE IV.—SANTA ANNA's quarters; present,
SANTA ANNA and FELISOLA.

[*Enter Officer, with flag.*]

SANTA ANNA.

What say the rebel dogs?
Dost cringe before my power, like spaniels
    whipped?
Or is their rebel flag pulled down,
And have they opened wide their gates,
That I may enter in,
And make my victory sure?

OFFICER.

Did'st hear that cannon's sound?
'Twas one of bold defiance sent,
The only answer they would give
To your demand. (*l*)

SANTA ANNA.

Hah! By the Virgin Mary, the Mother of Our
    Lord,
Their hearts shall quake, their hands shall pall,

Before my power, yet.
Here, see you to it,
That the red flag's run high up, (*e*)
Upon the church's dome, (*q*)
Where all may see it, and may know
That none, who thus my power brook,
Shall quarter have.

[Exit Officer.]

That blood red flag. I never ran
Upon its staff on high,
But some foul, traitorous blood was spilled,
To mark its stains with deeper dye;
And, lest the Virgin has withdrawn
Her favors far from me,
These traitors' blood before the dawn
Shall to its crimson added be;

[Turning to Felisola.]

And let the bugle sound,
To call the troops from quarters,
And have the fight begin, and make advance,
As best we may, to reach the walls in safety. (*l*)

[Exit Felisola.]

And shall I to *her* presence go?
Who has so much of magic power,
That e'en ambition folds its wings,
And treads with soft and silent step,
Within my heart, whilst she is near?
And my strong will does sway and bend,
Like tender stem, of spring time flower,
When touched, by passing zephyr's breath,
As her soft voice, in warning strikes my ear;
And I do then forget myself,
And my high aims, ambition's goal;

And if I'd follow where 'twould lead,
I'd sink to plane of other men,
Who are mere plodders in life's way.
And yet, so pleasing is the sense,
That though, like fowler's net,
With meshes strong,
It may me hold secure as prey.
I shun it not, but to her go,
And there again, I'll wend my way,
As I do need that magic power
To rid me of this choler;
And yet, I must from her still keep
The knowledge that she holds such power,
Lest a Delilah, she may be,
And I be made a Samson shorn.

Scene V.—Gen. Gaona's quarters; present,
Mrs. Gaona.
[*Enter Santa Anna.*]

MRS. GAONA.

What impulse brings you now to me?
Methinks your noble visage bears
Too plainly marks of anger.

SANTA ANNA.

Heed not that angry flush on brow,
It bodes no ill to you;
But rather temper now your speech
To drive that wrath away.

MRS. GAONA.

Pray, then, reveal the moving cause
For this, your shaded brow;

Aye, who so bold as but to dare
To give just cause for bringing there.

SANTA ANNA.

That traitor band within those walls,
The cause most just then gave,
When that defiant shot they sent,
As all the answer they would give
To my humane demand.

MRS. GAONA.

Hah! What is this I hear?
What form of message did you send,
They thus did dare to spurn?

SANTA ANNA.

'Twas such as that the world prescribes
'Tis meet to make by foe to foe,
When asking for surrender.

MRS. GAONA.

What terms did'st make you, in your offer?

SANTA ANNA.

Much better, e'en, than they deserve,
As they did lack conditions;
Whereas there should have gone with them
Some stringent form of penalty.

MRS. GAONA.

But if obeying your demand, what then?

SANTA ANNA.

Their lives would then be at my mercy.

MRS. GAONA.

Which, of a generous impulse born, you'd spare?

SANTA ANNA.

Nay, press me not, since what they've done
Puts all beyond contingencies,
And they the issue must abide.

MRS. GAONA.

Which you will cast in mercy's mould,
If you obtain the Virgin's favor.

SANTA ANNA.

'Tis not the Virgin, but the fate of war,
That holds now poised the issue.

MRS. GAONA.

And what does then the fate of war demand,
If you the victor?

SANTA ANNA.

If captured, then, to be all slain,
Such are the terms of this, our warfare.

MRS. GAONA.

Then, why be angered by refusal,
If there comes at best but forfeit;
And they, knowing such the terms,
Is it not far too much to look for,
That they'll yield without a struggle.

SANTA ANNA.

Then, that struggle they shall have
With such results as follow it;
And I must haste, and be away,
To press the battle I have ordered.

[*Exit Santa Anna.*]

MRS. GAONA.

O! Virgin Mother! Shield the brave,
Who battle for the right,
'Gainst such, ambition's wrong;
And I must, too, away,
To see what may be done,
If aught, to give them succor.

ACT IV.

Scene I.—Travis' quarters; present, Crock-ett, Evans, Dickinson and Bowie, the latter on his cot.

TRAVIS.

Companions in arms, I have called you to-
    gether in council,
As our straitened circumstances seem to de-
    mand it;
The foe has been gradually drawing closer
    upon us.
They have their batteries placed — one at the
    bridge, (*m*)
One on the Alamo ditch, to the northeast.
One at the powder-house,
And one at the old mill;
And we have, as you know, sustained
An uninterrupted bombardment,
For the last twenty-four hours; (*m*)
But, thank God, we have not lost a man,
And the flag of our country still proudly waves
Where we ourselves have placed it;
And while, like the noble 300 at Thermopylæ,
We have thrown ourselves into the breach,
For our country's cause, and, like them,
We may all, too, perish;
Yet, it would be worse than cowardly,

5

Not to struggle to the last;
I have dispatched Bonham
To Fannin, at Goliad, for assistance; (n)
I have sent urgent appeals
To those in authority over us.
Through these sources, succor may reach us yet,
But to ourselves we must at present look,
For possible prospects of deliverance,
And it is that we may make what may be to us
Our final and last arrangements for defence,
That this conference is called,
As we know not how soon the foe
May make an assault which may be successful,
Then, what we do must be done quickly;
As you know, our supply of provisions,
And much more, our ammunition, (q)
Is fast dwindling away;
And if an assult is made,
We have scarcely enough of the latter
To carry us through successfully
For the space of one day only,
If all our forces should be engaged therein.
Under this state of affairs,
What is the best to be done, is the question
For us to settle;
And what says Colonel Crockett?

CROCKETT.

Wall, now, Kernel, my old friend, Captain
    Scott, o' Varmount—
Perhaps you've hearn of him, Kernel—
Wall, he allers said "whar thar's life, thar's
    hope,"

And I, fer one, don't feel at arl
Like givin' up this har hunt;
No, Kernel, I cum har ter see it out,
And I'm gwine ter stik ter yer
Till ther last day in ther mornin',
And when ther last rooster's done his crowin',
Then I intend ter be thar,
Armed and equipped accordin' ter law,
As ther usenter have us ter do
When we war musterin'
In ther merlisher, in old Tennersee;
But them good old days
Am passed and gone, Kernel,
And, as ther poeter says,
We'll pass 'em by without ther sound o' a drum.
I must say, Kernel, yer speech has tuk
Arl the fine speechification outen me,
But I 'aint er gwine ter give it up so, Mister
   Brown;
No I 'aint, Kernel, and I'll wind up my speech
By sayin' ter yer, and arl ther boys,
That old DAVY CROCKETT will stick ter yer
As long as thar's a button on his old jenes coat.

[*Looking at and taking hold of his hunting
shirt.*]

Wall, Kernel, that's what I usenter say,
When I war speechifien in congress, yer see,
As that ar war ther kind I wore thar,
But this har ar nuthin' but my old huntin' shirt
Tied up with strings, with nary a button on it,
   Kernel,
But never mind, Kernel,

I'll stik ter yer all ther same,
So help me Moses, and that's ther same
As our Masonicer friends says
When they says "so mote it be."

MAJOR EVANS.

As the chief of ordnance,
It is proper, perhaps, I should say to you
That one reason of the scarcity
Of our supply of ammunition,
Was occasioned by there having been
A large part of the powder in the magazine
Damaged, from its leaky condition. (o)

CROCKETT.

That's it, Kernel, now I has it;
Yer see, if these 'ere blasted Greasers
Do cum hoopin' on ter us,
So as thar's no show fer a far fite,
Then let us stik a coal of fire
Rite dab inter that ar blasted old powder,
And blow 'em all to whar I torld my nabers
They might go ter when I cum ter Texas;
And if yer'll jist say ther word, Kernel,
Blast me, if I don't blow 'em higher ner a kite,
In less time than they could say Jack Rober-
     son twice;
Thar now, Kernel, that's my say agin.

TRAVIS.

Well, Colonel, your suggestion is a very good
     one, so far as it goes,
And if it be decreed that we shall be overcome,
I will take with you all this pledge:

That whoever may be left with strength and
    opportunity,
Shall touch off that powder, and by its explosion
Blow these glorious old walls down
Upon the heads of the foe. (*o*)

CROCKETT.

Blast me, if them 'aint my sentiments, 'zactly,
    Kernel.

TRAVIS.

And what say the rest?

CROCKETT.   •

O, don't ax 'em Kernel, fer yer knows
Thar 'aint one o' arl ther boys as would'nt glory
Ter see old Santer and arl his blasted pack
Flyin' higher nor Hamer—that ar feller
It tells erbout in ther good book, yer knows,
    Kernel,—
And I'll bet my bottom dollar thar's not one
    on 'em
Would ever git to that ar good place,
In goin' that ar way, neither;
And that's my say, agin, Kernel.

TRAVIS.

Well, let that be the pledge of all; (*o*)
And in order to make, as I have decided to do,
One last appeal and call
Upon the outside world for immediate aid,
I will dissolve the council,
And retire to my room for that purpose.

[*A scene is drawn, showing a room, into which
Travis enters and picks up some papers lying on
the table.*]

TRAVIS.

I had finished this before calling the council,
But lest I omitted something I should say,
I will read it over.

[*Reads.*]

" Fellow citizens and compatriots : (*p*)
I am besieged by a thousand, or more,
Of the Mexicans under SANTA ANNA.
I have sustained a continuous bombardment
For twenty-four hours,
And have not lost a man.
The enemy have demanded a surrender at
    discretion,
Otherwise the garrison is to be put to the sword,
If the place is taken.
I have answered the summons with a cannon
    shot,
And our flag still waves proudly from our walls;
I shall never surrender, or retreat.
Then, I call on you in the name of Liberty, of
    Patriotism,
And everything dear to the American character,
To come to our aid with all dispatch.
The enemy are receiving reinforcements daily,
And will no doubt increase
To three or four thousand in four or five days.
Though this call may be neglected,
I am determined to sustain myself
As long as possible,
And die like a soldier, who never forgets
What is due to his own honor,
And that of his country—
Victory, or death !"

And this I've added, by way of postscript :
" The Lord is on our side.
When the enemy appeared in sight,
We had not three bushels of corn ;
We have since found, in deserted houses
Eighty or ninety bushels,
And gotten into the walls
Twenty or thirty head of beeves."
And this I must, with all dispatch,
Send off unto our friends ;
But on their failure to respond, what then ?
This now our foe, with o'erwhelming force,
And come, as he has done, to place
The last strong chain upon the nation,
Does, with bold arrogance, demand
That we surrender at discretion ;
And which refused, he still by force
Would make us it obey ;
And armed, too, with that foul decree,
Which he his pliant congress made
Through forms alone of law,
Bear impress of their sanction,
And what would such surrender be,
But death or slavery ?
For but as pirates, as decreed,
With one so base to it enforce,
What hope have we for quarter ?
The lamb from wolf might better look
For freedom and security.
No, our purpose taken,
We'll here abide the issue of the contest. (*r*)
And my own heart I must relieve

By making some provision for my *boy.*
I have a friend in Washington,
To whom I will this note dispatch,
Which let me read, since I penned it
With so much then of feeling,
I know not if it does contain
What I then meant to say.

[*He reads.*]

" Take care of my little boy ; (*q*)
If the country should be saved,
I may make him a splendid fortune;
But if the country should be lost,
And I should perish,
He will have nothing
But the proud recollection
That he is the son of a man
Who died for his country;"

[*Folding the papers.*]

And I must these dispatches place,
Within some trusty hand,
To have them reach their destination.

SCENE II.—SANTA ANNA'S quarters; a table,
with a drum upon it; SANTA ANNA walking back
and forth; time, late in the evening.

SANTA ANNA.

I do so chafe, from this restraint of mine,
That I do fear me,
Like the bit to horse's mouth,
It will my spirit make so callous,
I'll ne'er again feel tender touch
With which to guide me

To ambition's height.
See how that small, defiant band,
Cooped up by my vast force,
Within those walls of stone,
Doth check ambition's flight.
For they alone my way hedge up,
And but for them
My rule would be supreme;
Why, then, do I so tamely yield
To this, my self-imposed restraint;
For what, save my own will, prevents me now
From crushing out by force
This barrier in my way?
But prudence, ah! thou dost for aye,
Thy silent whisp'rings bid me hear;
And hearing, I have heeded now,
'Till patience hath of woof so small
That it is threadbare.
And yet, one effort more I'll make
To calm thy clamors,
And will a council call,
That I may its poor sanction have
For what I might without it do —
This one obstruction here remove
To my ambition.
Then, I will strike, and orders give
To have the council called.

[*He strikes the drum, and a sentinel enters.*]

The members summon here forthwith,
That form my council;
And bid them come without delay,
As I have business urgent.   [*Exit Sentinel.*]

Ah! With myself to hold commune,
And fathom all the depths to which
This degredation leads me,
And then to soar to where I'd rise
By height of my ambition;
'Tis more of strain than long I'll bear,
This is my last submission.

[*Enter Felisola, Cos, Castrillon, Ramirez, Sesma and Almonta.*]

SANTA ANNA.

A task imposed, a burden laid,
Is this my call upon you,
Since but to sanction what is plain
My duty bids that I should do,
I've called you thus together.
Those rebels, as you are aware,
Their lives did then there forfeit
By that defiant answer sent
From cannon's mouth to my demand;
And what doth hindrance make that I
Should pour my force upon them,
And like the Red Sea, as of old,
Their force o'erwhelm and swallow up?
Should mingling streams of blood deter
Of victors and the vanquished slain?
What flower upon the earth does bloom,
But owes its life to some decay;
And where has yet there been e'er reared
A power to rule o'er man's estate
Except that blood to it was brought
A holocaust, or sacrifice?
But as before I did submit

To you, as council, what to do,
I have it deemed still best of you
To ask what shall by me be done.
Shall I assail by bold assault,
Or shall I by degrees approach?
What say you all?
Those who the first to counsel would,
Their places take here, on my right;
And they the other would approve,
Their places take upon my left.

[*They divide, with Ramirez, Sesma and Almonta on the right, and Felisola, Cos and Castrillon on the left.*]

SANTA ANNA.

'Tis well the council so divides, (*s*)
Decision yet with me remains,   -
And I will, ere the morrow dawns,
My own decision then have made;
And to your stations you may go,
And there await the coming morn,
As it shall to you then reveal my will.

[*Exit all but Santa Anna.*]

O, fate! O, providence, or whatsoe'er thou art,
That dost our destinies control,
To thee I here would pay my court,
And pray thee be propitious;
The sun's bright ray that first shall cast
His beams athwart yon eastern sky,
Shall bear a message unto me,
To build ambition's hopes upon,
Or bear them down to earth,

As I the gage of battle will
Ere that have full thrown down; (*t*)
And on the issue hangs my fate
To be a ruler over all,
Or menial be to strong restraint;
And I must to her once more go,
And carry this, my burden.

SCENE III.—Gen. GAONA's quarters; present,
Mrs. GAONA.   [*Enter Santa Anna.*]

MRS. GAONA.

What! The honor do you seek,
To thus upon me now confer;
Or what the burden would you lighten
By this coming of your's here.

SANTA ANNA.

Like the shadows that are falling,
Bringing on the night, now near,
The veil that is the future hiding,
Does obstruct our anxious peer.
The will hath gained my purpose over
To the foe at once assault,
And I the plan to you uncover,
To approve, or yet find fault;
Since, perforce by wisdom, woman
Does the future oft reveal,
And if it be not from you hidden,
I pray you not from me conceal;
Since my council called divided,
And decision left to me,
I to make assault, decided,
Would your counsel thus, too, be?

MRS. GAONA.

The zephyr's breath soft whisp'ring sounds,
From forest leaves, do oft us bring,
But when the thunder clap resounds,
The very vaults of Heaven ring;
And shall the still, small voice be heard,
From woman's cautious counsel given;
What to ambition's ears her word,
Though it convey the will of Heaven.

SANTA ANNA.

Hah! Would you have my hand to stay
From shedding those foul traitors' blood;
Or, do you counsel better way
Than by assault to be, there would?

MRS. GAONA.

Nay; I no counsel would you give;
I did but answer to your will.
For what we do ourselves believe,
Though counsel 'gainst, we hold, too, still.

SANTA ANNA.

Then it is fixed, the purpose formed,
And in the coming dawn they'll see
Their boasted shield of stone walls stormed
By cannon and with infantry. (*t*)

      [*Exit Santa Anna.*]

MRS. GAONA.

Ah, well I knew, his purpose fixed,
'Twould folly be to say him nay;
And I will haste and them apprise
Of what awaits them in the morn.

Scene IV.—*Storming of the Alamo*, with noise of the battle outside. The two Mexican women hurry on to the stage, accompanied by Mrs. Gaona dressed in male attire, and when the two enter a door (which should represent the entrance to one of the cells in the wall) and it is closed behind them. Mrs. Gaona takes from her pocket the necessary badges to complete a Colonel's uniform, and attaches them to the suit she has on, then she draws out a sword she had concealed on her person.]

MRS. GAONA.

These will serve to shield me from detection,
And I must see what can be done, if aught,
To serve them.

[*Exit Mrs. Gaona.*]

[*As soon as she is off the stage, Travis' negro servant comes running on, and, looking wildly, runs around upon the stage.*]

SERVANT.

O, Massa Travis! Massa Travis! Massa Travis!
They have killed Massa Travis,
And they will kill me;
Whar shall I go? Whar shall I go?
What shall I do? What shall I do?

[*At which time he comes opposite the door through which the Mexican women entered, who having opened it, he darts in, and it is closed behind him. Mrs. Dickinson then comes running on, carrying her child.*]

STORMING OF THE ALAMO.

MRS. DICKINSON.

O, my God! what shall I do?
They have gotten over the wall;
They are killing the men—
They will kill my husband!
They will kill us all.
O, my child, my child,
What shall I do? What shall I do?
O, God, have mercy upon us.

[*The two Mexican women rush out and drag her in and close the door behind them. (n) A scene is then drawn, showing Bowie on his cot, resting half reclining, supported on his left elbow, with an empty pistol in his right hand, which he throws away and lies down on his cot, when two Mexicans with fixed bayonets approach and are in the act of thrusting them into him, when Mrs. Gaona, in her Colonel's uniform comes up, and throws up their guns with her sword.*]

MRS. GAONA.

Hold, there, ye craven coward dogs,
Would you dare strike a foe unarmed,
You'd put the savage beasts to shame,
That spare the sick and wounded prey.
Begone, ye cowards! Off! Away!
And seek a stalwart foe,
With strength of arm, backed by a will,
To pit against your own.

[*Enter Santa Anna.*]

6

SANTA ANNA.

Hah!   What have we here?
Who is so bold, as by command to dare
To supreme orders disobey,
And e'en one traitor's life to spare?

[*Turning to Soldiers.*]

This Gringo dog at once dispatch,
And supreme orders thus obey.

[*They thrust their bayonets into Bowie, and
Santa Anna, turning to Mrs. Gaona, says to
soldiers.*]

And, here, this traitor closely guard,
And to the guard house take
To for this daring act he's done,
To answer a court martial.

[*They start off with her one way, and Santa
Anna goes another.   A scene is then drawn,
showing a room, which should represent the magazine, with a pile of old powder in view, into
which Evans enters.*]

MAJOR EVANS.

And, is it true the rest have fallen,
And I have been by Heaven spared,
To here redeem the pledge as given,
And vengeance take upon the foe?
The noble TRAVIS, as he manned the gun,
Upon the western wall,
To thus relieve the exhausted men,
Received the deadly shot, and there expired;
And, as we came upon the wall,
To repel the invading host,

Where they pressed on us the hardest,
The gallant BONHAM and DICKINSON
Fell before their murderous fire ;
And as I came hither,
I passed BOWIE on his cot, with life extinct,
And CROCKETT, I know not of him. ;
But if fallen, he has not spared the foe,
But has demanded life for life, by many fold ;
And those, our other comrades in arms,
All, all, have given their lives for their country.
A noble band of martyrs! Oh, sacred Alamo,
Thou shalt go down in history with Thermopylæ

[He hears a noise from without.]

Hah! Hear how they yet pour in,
Like beasts of prey around their victims,
When the scent of blood is wafted on the breeze,
But now they shall themselves be made the
    victims,
As vengeance shall be meted out to them,
Since Providence does will it so.

[Turning to the pile of old powder.]

And thou trash! Thou more than trash!
For thou didst mock us,
When we would have loaded thee within our
    guns ;
But now, thou shalt be made a Samson of,
To bring these glorious old walls all down
Upon the heads of these Philistian foes of Texas
And oh, thou sacred Alamo!
That thou shouldst be made a heap of ruins,
And I, even I, the Heaven-favored one,
To make thee so.

And come, ye spirits of my dead comrades,
And witness here the fulfillment of my vow,
As I shall touch this pile of powder off,
And thus take vengeance on the foe.

[*He strikes his flint and steel, and stoops down
to put his lighted tinder to the powder.*]

O God, receive my spirit!

[*A shot is fired through the door, and he falls
away from the powder and a Mexican enters and
bayonets him. Another scene is then drawn,
showing Crockett pursued by the Mexicans, when
he takes up a position in the angle of the wall,
with his back to it, (o) and with his gun clubbed,
he wields it furiously.*]

CROCKETT.

Bring on yer lioners and tigers,
Yer cattermounts and allergaters,
Fer I'm er half hoss and half allergater my-
    self, I ar;
Bring on yer sea hoss, yer red hoss, and yer
    land tarrapin,
Yer white bar, yer black bar, and yer grizler
    bar,
Yer big fish, yer leetle fish, and yer whales,
Yer boer-constricters, yer snappin' turtles and
    tad poles,
Yer black-and-tans, yer grey hounds, and yer
    terriers,
Yer bob-tail cats, yer long-tail cats, and yer
    ring-tail roarers,
Fer I'm ther he-coon uv ther valleys,
And ther she-coon uv ther ridges;

I'm ther old eriginal zip-coon,
And that uther coon er sottin' on er rail;
And I'm that same old coon
What allers war er coon,
And that never got er lickin' till yet.

[*One of them gets up close enough to punch him.*]

And that's ther way yer puts in yer licks, ar it?

[*Crockett knocks him down with his gun.*]

And zip I tuk yer, and now pitch in, thar,
With yer double-shuffle, pigeon-wing,
And all-fours, too;
With yer double-quick, and turn erbout,
And do jist so.
With yer whisker-toddies,
Lemonade and soder-water, too,
And yer don't know who yer tryin' ter lick,
Now does yer?

[*Another one gets up close enough to stick him.*]

Hip, hurra! now let me see yer try ter do that
ar ergin.

[*He knocks him down.*]

Now I haz yer; zip, I tuk yer.
Cum on, thar, with yer eaglers,
And yer ostrichers and buzzards,
With yer bed-bugs and yer fire-flies,
Yer snakes and yer grass-hoppers.
Bring all creation with yer,
And I'll whoop yer up together,
Like hot soup on er ladle-handle,
Or a slidin' on greased lightnin;

And yer don't know who you're tryin' ter lick
  now, does yer?

[*Another one sticks him and he knocks him down*]

Now, hip, hurra! kerzip, yer tuk me;
Now I has yer; zip, I tuk yer.

> [*Several of them crowd upon him.*]

Whoopee, thar; Greenland! Christmas!
Sunday, Monday—any day but this.

> [*He knocks another one down.*]

And now yer has it; zip, I tuk yer.

> [*Another one gives him a thrust.*]

Gerusalem, Tom Payne,
And all ther tother saints!
And I say, yer don't know who yer tryin' ter
  lick now, does yer?

> [*He knocks him down.*]

And now yer has it; zip, I tuk yer.
Git up thar afore day in ther morin' will yer?
And wipe out all yer eyes out thar, will yer?

> [*Several of them make a rush at him.*]

Gershoserfat! and yer don't know
Who yer tryin' ter lick now, does yer?

> [*Enter Santa Anna.*]

SANTA ANNA.

Ho, here! what now? would the lamb the wolf,
Or kid the lion put to bay?
Base, coward wretches, strike!

Your arms there wield,
And this last foe despatch,
That I may rule supreme.

[Crockett, seeing him come up without any arms, and not understanding what he is saying, but thinking he wants to take up the fight himself, and not wishing to have the advantage, sets his gun down in the corner behind him and puts his coon-skin cap beside it, which action throws the Mexican soldiers off their guard as well as arrests the attention of Santa Anna. Then Crockett begins taking off his hunting-shirt, which when done, he rolls up his sleeves, according to the old Tennessee method, and while he is doing all this he is going over with :]

CROCKETT.

What's that ar yer gittin' through yer thar,
    old coon?
Yer wants ter tuk up this har fite yerself, does
    yer?
A far and squar fiite—no bitin' ner gougin',
Ner no dorg falls—then I'm yer man, I ar;
But maber so, yer don't know
Who 'tis yer wants ter lick, does yer?
Wall, then I'll tell yer.
It ar old DAVY CROCKETT, o' Tennersee, it ar.
And yer wants ter tuk up
This har fite yerself, does yer?

[Then, with a wave of the hand to the others.]

Thar, flank 'round thar, little ones,
And let me pitch inter him

Like a thousand o' brick;
I'll show an old blab-mouthed blatherskite
    like him
How ter come 'round har
And tuk up uther folks' fites, I will.
Whoopee, thar! look out thar, old coon,
I'm a cummin', I ar!
And now squar yerself,
Fer kerzip, I'll tuk yer!

*[He spits on his hands, and leaps over the
bodies around him, in the direction of Santa
Anna, when he is knocked down by the soldiers,
and bayoneted.]*

COL. WILLIAM McLANE,

Who died at his residence, at the head of the San Antonio river, adjoining the city limits of San Antonio, Texas, May 11th, 1873, and who was the last of the Magee expedition, which expedition aided materially in securing the freedom of Mexico from Spanish rule, and which ultimately led to the independence of Texas, and the account of which expedition, as penned by himself, is embodied in a 400-page work now in press by the San Antonio Printing Co., entitled "IRENE VIESCA, A TALE OF THE MAGEE EXPEDITION, IN THE GAUCHIPIN WAR IN TEXAS, IN 1812-13;" and by the author of the present work.

APPENDIX.

EXTRACTS FROM YOAKUM'S HISTORY OF TEXAS.

The following extracts are taken from *Yoakum's History of Texas*, and are inserted here with corresponding reference marks to those employed in the body of the work, to show the inquiring reader—who may not be familiar with the history, and to save those who are, the trouble of hunting them out—the particular passages to which the author of the present work is indebted for the foundations upon which to construct it. And it will be seen that he has followed as closely the facts as the nature and scope of the work would warrant. The parts assigned GENERAL and MRS. GAONA being the only departures from a strict adherance to the actual facts of history. Her part being assigned her to meet a general demand for some leading female character in all works of the kind. And while the part assigned her might have been repugnant to her loyalty to Santa Anna, as well as to her womanly modesty, yet, as we have taken the liberty we have with her, we can only make amend by giving this explanation and offering this our suitable apology. The selection of GEN. GAONA as a friend of the Texans was not altogether unwarranted, from the fact that he disapproved of much that Santa Anna did in his dealings with the Texans.

(a) In the meantime, Santa Anna was engaged in Mexico in the consolidation of a despotism. There were in that nation many genuine friends of liberty, ardent supporters of the con-

stitution of 1824; but the terrors of banishment and death restrained them. Those who dared to oppose him were pursued and hunted down, like wild beasts. Of this number were Zavalla and Mexia. The congress was completely in his hands. With the clergy and the army he fulminated his spiritual and military thunders. Over a timid and superstitious people his power had become nearly omnipotent. All but Texas had bowed the neck to the imperious tyrant. To him she was like ' Mordecai sitting in the king's gate.' His plan for her subjugation was, however, skilfully laid. It was to fill the country gradually with military forces, under different pretences. In fact, five hundred troops were embarked for Texas in April of the present year (1835), but disturbances in Zacatecas caused them to be recalled. The time which the dictator had fixed for the overthrow of the constitution was in the following October. Events had, however, hurried him on so rapidly, that he was compelled to change his plan, and dispatch troops to Texas more rapidly. In July he accordingly sent two hundred and fifty; in the first days of August three hundred more; and there were a thousand more on the route.—Page 351; Vol. I.

By the month of August it was clearly understood that the federal constitution was to be destroyed. The plan of Toluca— countenanced, and perhaps started by Santa Anna—proposed a central government. The doctrine had already gone forth that the authority of the national congress was unlimited—that it could do anything which Santa Anna desired. It was farther understood that the president was to hold his office for eight years, and was to have some sort of advisory body, a council or congress, but this body was to be dependent on him.—Page 352; Vol. I.

* * * Santa Anna asked for opium. A piece of about five grains was handed him, which he swallowed. He immediately proposed to enter into negotiations for his liberation, but General Houston answered him that it was a subject of which he could not take cognizance, inasmuch as Texas had a government to which such matters appropriately belonged. Santa Anna observed that he disliked to have anything to do with civilians; that he abhorred them, and would much rather treat with the general of the army. "And," continued he, "General, you can afford to be generous; you are born to no common destiny—you have conquered the Napoleon of the west." * * * General

Houston then asked him how he expected to negotiate under the circumstances that had occurred at the Alamo. About this time Colonel Almonte, who had been sent for, arrived, and after salutations between him and his chief, the latter replied that "General Houston knew that, by the rules of war, when a fortress, insufficient to defend itself, was summoned to surrender and refused and caused the effusion of human blood, the vanquished, when it was taken, were devoted to execution." General Houston replied that "he knew such to have been the rule at one period, but he thought it now obsolete, and a disgrace to the nineteenth century." "But," continued Houston, "General Santa Anna, you can not urge the same excuse for the massacre at Goliad. *They* capitulated, were betrayed, and massacred in cold blood." Santa Anna replied: "If they ever had capitulated he was not aware of it. Urrea had deceived him, and informed him that they were vanquished; and he had orders from his government to execute all that were taken with arms in their hands." Houston rejoined: "General Santa Anna, you are the government — a dictator has no superior." "But," answered Santa Anna, "I have the order of our congress to treat all that were found with arms in their hands resisting the authority of the government, as pirates. And Urrea has deceived me. He had no authority to enter into any agreement; and if I ever live to regain power he shall be punished for it.—Pages 147, 148 and 149; Vol. II.

(*b*) In the meantime, early in July, Lorenzo de Zavalla, late governor of the State and City of Mexico, and embassador to France, had fled from the tyranny of Santa Anna and sought refuge on the shores of Texas. No sooner had the Mexican authorities learned this fact than an order was dispatched to have him arrested.—Page 344; Vol. I.

Santa Anna was extremely solicitous to obtain possession of the person of Zavalla. The latter had been his friend, and had sustained him in a trying hour. But the aid was given for the cause of liberty! Santa Anna had deserted that cause, and now wished to sacrifice an ancient friend, who might live to reproach him for his perfidy. 'I give this supreme order,' says Tornell to Cos, 'having the honor to direct to you, requiring you to provide and bring into action all your ingenuity and activity in arranging energetic plans for success in the apprehension of Don Lorenzo Zavalla, which person, in the actual circumstances of Texas, must be very pernicious. To this end, I particularly recommend that you spare no means to secure his person, and place it at the disposition of the supreme government.' Cos, in transmitting this order to Ugartachea, on the 8th of August, directed him, if Zavalla was not given up, to proceed, at the head of all his cavalry, to execute the command, and to give to the local authorities on the route, information as to his sole object.—Pages 347–348; Vol. I.

(c) General Santa Anna, the Mexican president, having determined to lead the invading army in person, reached Saltillo in January, where, for a time, he made his headquarters. On the 1st of February, he set out for the Rio Grande, by way of Monclova, with a force of six thousand men. He reached the river on the 12th, where he halted till the 16th, waiting for the troops to come up, and to make suitable preparations for crossing the uninhabited prairies which lay between him and Bexar. While tarrying at Guerrero, he was engaged in dictating to the central government his views as to the policy to be pursued towards Texas, when it should be reduced. His plan was as follows: To drive from the province all who had taken part in the revolution, together with all foreigners who lived near the sea coast, or the borders of the United States; to remove far into the interior those who had not taken part in the war; to vacate all sales and grants of land owned by non-residents; to remove from Texas all who had come to the province, and were not entered as colonists under Mexican rules; to divide among the officers and soldiers of the Mexican army the best lands, provided they would occupy them; to permit no Anglo-American to settle in Texas; to sell the remaining vacant lands at one dollar per acre —allowing the French to buy only five millions of acres, the English the same, the Germans somewhat more, and to those speaking the Spanish language, without limit; to satisfy the claims of the civilized Indians; to make the Texans pay the expenses of the war; and to liberate and declare free the negroes introduced into the province.—Pages 64–65; Vol. II.

(d) Here are the decrees referred to by Santa Anna:

"1. Foreigners, landing on the coast of the Republic, or invading its territory by land, armed, and with the intention of attacking our country, will be deemed *pirates*, and dealt with as such, being citizens of no nation presently at war with the Republic, and fighting under no recognized flag.

" 2. All foreigners, who shall import, by either sea or land, in the places occupied by the rebels, either arms or ammunition of any kind, for their use, will be deemed *pirates*, and punished as such.

" I send you these decrees, that you may cause them to be fully executed.

"TORNEL.

"MEXICO, December 30, 1835."—Note on page ᵢ49, Vol. II.

" *To General Urrea, Commanding, Etc.:*

[Official.]

" In respect to the prisoners, of whom you speak in your last communication, you must not fail to bear in mind the circular of the supreme government, in which it is decreed that foreigners invading the Republic, and taken with arms in their hands, shall be judged and treated as pirates; and as, in my view of the matter, every Mexican guilty of the crime of joining these adventurers, loses the rights of a citizen by his unnatural conduct, the five Mexican prisoners, whom you have taken, ought also to suffer as traitors.

[Unofficial.]

" In regard to foreigners, who make war, and those unnatural Mexicans, who have joined their cause, you will remark, that what I have stated to you officially is in accordance with the former provisions of the supreme government. An example is necessary, in order that these adventurers may be duly warned, and the nation be delivered from the ills she is daily doomed to suffer.

"ANTONIO LOPEZ DE SANTA ANNA.

" GENERAL QUARTERS, BEXAR, March 3, 1836."

" *To General Urrea, Commanding, Etc.:*

" Under date of the present, I have stated to the commandant of the Post of Goliad, as follows:

" By a communication, made to me by Colonel D. F. Gray, of that place, I am informed that there have been sent to you by General Urrea, 234 prisoners, taken in the action of *Encinal del Perdido* (Coleta), on the 19th and 20th of the present month; and as the supreme government has ordered that all foreigners, taken with arms in their hands, making war upon the nation, shall be treated as pirates, I have been surprised that the circular of the said supreme government has not been fully complied with in this particular. *I therefore order, that you should give immediate effect to the said ordinance in respect to all those for-*

eigners who have yielded to the force of arms, having had the audacity to come and insult the Republic, to devastate with fire and sword, as has been the case in Goliad, causing vast detriment to our citizens; in a word, shedding the precious blood of Mexican citizens, whose only crime has been fidelity to their country. I trust that, in reply to this, you will inform me that *public vengeance has been satisfied* by the punishment of such detestable delinquents. I transcribe the said decree of the government for your guidance, and that you may strictly fulfill the same, in the zealous hope that, for the future, the provisions of the supreme government may not, for a moment, be infringed.

"ANTONIO LOPEZ DE SANTA ANNA.

"HEADQUARTERS BEXAR, March 23, 1836."—pp. 516–517, Vol. II.

(*e*) * * Cos and his officers were permitted to retire with their arms and private property, upon their word of honor that they would not, in any way, oppose the re-establishment of the constitution of 1824; the Mexican convict soldiers were to be taken beyond the Rio Grande. * * It is proper here to state that during the attack, notwithstanding General Burleson had out a constant patrol, Ugartachea made his way into San Antonio with five hundred convicts, guarded by a hundred regular infantry.—Pages 30–31; Vol. II.

(*f*) We have seen the preparations of the contending forces, and have followed Santa Anna, with a well appointed army, to the walls of Bexar, and Urrea to San Patricio. We have seen Travis, with some thirty men, sent by Governor Smith to the former place, and Bowie dispatched by Houston, with a like number, from Goliad. One other worthy is yet lacking to take part in the death struggle at the Alamo. David Crockett was a Tennesseean. His education, which consisted mostly in the fearless rifle, he had himself acquired in the then unsettled forests of West Tennessee. Having strong natural powers of mind, he was elected to the State Legislature, and subsequently as representative to Congress. But he did not comprehend the machinery of the federal government. The rules of Jefferson's manual were to him as mysterious as the Delphian oracles. Hence, his efforts in the House of Representatives were abortive, and so notoriously so, that he was not returned. The struggle then pending in Texas was more to his taste, and he came to take part in it.